MW00837885

FLYING
SQUIRRELS

by Judith Jango-Cohen

Pull Ahead Books

Lerner Publications Company • Minneapolis

Dedicated to Laura Waxman, editor, with thanks and best wishes.

A special thank you to Trinity Muller, photo researcher, for assembling this amazing array of flying squirrel images.

This book is available in two editions:
Library binding by Lerner Publications Company, a division of Lerner Publishing Group
Soft cover by First Avenue Editions, an imprint of Lerner Publishing Group
241 First Avenue North
Minneapolis, MN 55401 U.S.A.

Website address: www.lernerbooks.com

Words in *italic* type are explained in a glossary on page 30.

Library of Congress Cataloging-in-Publication Data

Jango-Cohen, Judith.
    Flying squirrels / by Judith Jango-Cohen.
        p.   cm. — (Pull ahead books)
    Includes index.
    Summary: Introduces the physical characteristics, behavior, and habitats of flying squirrels.
    ISBN: 0-8225-3772-9 (lib. bdg. : alk. paper)
    ISBN: 0-8225-9886-8 (pbk. : alk. paper)
    1. Flying squirrels—Juvenile literature. [1. Flying squirrels. 2. Squirrels.] I. Title. II. Series.
QL737.R68J36 2004
599.36'9—dc21   2003002312

Manufactured in the United States of America
1 2 3 4 5 6 — JR — 09 08 07 06 05 04

Most people have never seen
a flying squirrel.

Do you know why?

A flying
squirrel
stays tucked
in its *nest*
and naps
all day.

Its nest may be a hole
inside an old tree.

Or its nest may be a heap of twigs,
bark, and leaves.

Flying squirrels are *nocturnal*.

Nocturnal animals are active at night.

Flying squirrels are hungry
when they get up.

They hunt for *buds*, seeds, nuts,
and bugs.

Sometimes they look for food while hanging by the claws on their feet.

A flying squirrel must travel from tree to tree to find its food.

How does it get from one tree to the next?

First, the squirrel takes a good look at the next tree.

It bobs up and down.
It leans from side to side.

Then it spreads its front
and back feet and glides.

Flaps of skin help the flying squirrel glide. The skin is called the *patagium*.

It stretches tight like a mighty sail.

The squirrel tucks in its feet when it reaches the tree.

The patagium folds up. The squirrel's sharp claws dig into the bark.

Then the flying squirrel scurries out of sight.

It tries to hide in case an owl is watching.

Owls are *predators* of flying squirrels.

Predators are animals that hunt and eat other animals.

House cats try to catch
flying squirrels, too.

But flying squirrels have large eyes. Their eyes watch for predators.

When the woods look safe,
flying squirrels come out.

Spring, summer, and fall are busy times for flying squirrels.

They glide, hide, scurry, hurry, hunt, and eat.

Winter is not as busy a time.

Flying squirrels do not go out
as much when it is cold.

They come out only to find nuts that they hid in the fall.

They cuddle in their nests to keep warm until spring.

In the spring, *pups* are born.
Pups are baby flying squirrels.

New pups are skinny and pink.
Soon they will grow fur.

Flying squirrels are *mammals*.
Baby mammals drink mother's milk.

The mother squirrel's patagium
covers her pups like a silky quilt.

When the pups are five weeks old,
they squeak and play in the nest.

Their mother has to stay outside
to get some rest.

Older pups play outside.
Sometimes one falls.

Then the mother picks up her pup.
The pup curls into a fluffy ball.

Flying squirrels may live near you.

Have you seen them?

Set out some seeds and nuts
at night, and you might.

KEY:

▨ shows where flying squirrels live

Find your state or province on this map.
Do flying squirrels live near you?

Parts of a Flying Squirrel's Body

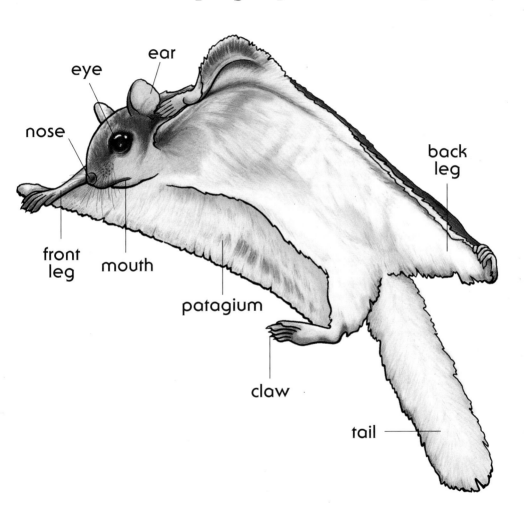

eye

ear

nose

back
leg

front
leg

mouth

patagium

claw

tail

Glossary

buds: small, new parts of a plant that grow into a leaf or flower

mammals: animals that drink their mother's milk

nest: a safe place where a flying squirrel sleeps, rests, and eats

nocturnal: to be active at night

patagium: loose skin on a flying squirrel that helps it glide

predators: animals that hunt and eat other animals

pups: baby flying squirrels

Hunt and Find

The publisher wishes to extend special thanks to our **series consultant,** Sharyn Fenwick. An elementary science-math specialist, Mrs. Fenwick was the recipient of the National Science Teachers Association 1991 Distinguished Teaching Award. In 1992, representing the state of Minnesota at the elementary level, she received the Presidential Award for Excellence in Math and Science Teaching.

Eliot Cohen

About the Author

"Watching squirrels is always fun," says Judith Jango-Cohen. "But listening to squirrels can be helpful." When Judith and her husband Eliot were hiking in Canada, a chorus of ground squirrels began peeping. A grizzly bear and two cubs were coming! Thanks to the squirrels, Judith and Eliot saw the bears and quickly left the area. Now whenever squirrels in their yard knock over bird feeders, Judith never gets too mad at them. She lives in Burlington, Massachusetts, with her family, surrounded by trees and tricky squirrels.

Photo Acknowledgments

The photographs in this book are reproduced with permission from: © Steve and Dave Maslowski, cover, pp. 4, 6, 7, 10, 11, 15, 18, 20, 25, 27; © Rob Simpson/Visuals Unlimited, p. 3; © Erwin and Peggy Bauer/Tom Stack & Associates, pp. 5, 24; © Joe McDonald, pp. 8, 19, 26, 31; © William Weber/Visuals Unlimited, pp. 9, 21; © Maslowski Photo/Visuals Unlimited, pp. 12, 13; © Joe McDonald/Visuals Unlimited, p. 14; © Trinity Muller/Independent Picture Service, p. 16; © Rob & Ann Simpson/Visuals Unlimited, p. 17; © Bill Beatty/Visuals Unlimited, p. 22; © Nancy M. Wells/Visuals Unlimited, p. 23.